To my great-granddaughters Charlotte Rebecca Burrows and Olivia Burrows – S.I.
For Michael and Eira – A.C.L.

First published in Great Britain in 2000 by Bloomsbury Publishing Plc
38 Soho Square, London, W1D 3HB
This paperback edition first published 2001

A CIP catalogue record of this book is available from the British Library
ISBN 0 7475 5053 0 (Paperback)
ISBN 0 7475 4479 4 (Hardback)

Designed by Dawn Apperley

Printed in Hong Kong by South China Printing Co

1 3 5 7 9 10 8 6 4 2

Flora the Frog

Shirley Isherwood and Anna C Leplar

BLOOMSBURY
CHILDREN'S
BOOKS

Flora's class was going to give a play. It was to be about creatures who lived in a wood. All the children in the class were very excited. Miss Brown clapped her hands. 'Quiet everyone!' she said.

'Now I will tell everyone which part they will have in the play.
John, you will be a fox.'
'I want to be an elephant,' said John.
'There are no elephants in a wood,' said Miss Brown firmly.
'You will be a fox.'

'Katie, you will be a squirrel.' Katie smiled, for she liked squirrels.
'James, you will be a rabbit.' James was pleased. He kept two rabbits at home, and knew just how they hopped, and twitched their noses.
'But we must have some trees, too,' said Miss Brown. 'Who would like to be a tree?'
Some of the children put up their hands.
'Good!' said Miss Brown.

And then she turned to Flora. 'Flora,' she said, 'you will be a frog.' Flora thought, 'I don't want to be a frog.' But she didn't say anything.

When it was time to go home, she ran to the gate. Her mother
and Aunt Jo were waiting for her.
'I'm in the class play,' said Flora. 'I'm a frog.'
'How wonderful!' said her mother. 'I was a fairy in my class play.
I had beautiful gauzy wings.'
'I was an elf in my class play,' said Aunt Jo. 'I had pointy shoes
with bells on the toes. I loved being an elf.'

'I'll make you a lovely frog costume,' said Flora's mother.

'I'll help you,' said Aunt Jo.

'We'll make long green legs,' said Flora's mother.

'And a fat green tummy,' said Aunt Jo.

Flora wished that she could be a fairy with wings, or an elf with bells on her toes.

The next morning, the costume was ready. 'Take it to school to show the children and Miss Brown,' said Flora's mother. She folded the frog and put it in a bag.

As Flora hurried along with her mother, she saw that one of the frog's hands was hanging over the rim of the bag. It flipped up and down, as though it were waving to her. Flora bundled it back inside the bag.

When Flora reached the playground, she saw that Daisy, Katie, James and John were together, practising being the animals in the play.

'They're all something nice,' thought Flora, 'and I'm just a fat green frog. I don't want to be a frog.'

She looked round, and when she thought that no one was looking, she took the frog costume from the bag, and threw it up into a tree. It hung over a branch and just the tip of one of its hands could be seen, peeping from the leaves.

All morning, Flora looked through the window, and saw the frog's hand. It swayed to and fro in the tree, as though it were waving to her again.

In the afternoon, the children rehearsed their play. Everyone tried very hard to be good in their part – except Flora. 'I don't want to do it,' she said.

'But, why, Flora?' asked her teacher. 'I picked you to be the frog because you jump so well. You can jump higher than anyone else.'

Flora said nothing. She thought, 'If I said that everyone is something nice and I'm just a fat green frog, everyone will laugh at me.' She marched to her desk and sat down.
Glancing through the window, she saw that the hand had stopped waving. It was almost as if the frog had heard what she said.

'Did everyone like your frog costume?' asked Flora's mother at teatime.

'Yes,' said Flora. She finished her tea, took her ball, and went out to play. Her mother and Aunt Jo sat by the window, and watched her. Flora knew that they had guessed that something was wrong. She felt awful. She had thrown the frog costume into a tree, and she'd told a lie.

'Why couldn't someone else have been a frog!' she thought angrily, and threw the ball so hard that it bounced over the fence, and into the garden next door.
There was a gap in the fence, and Flora slipped through.

She ran across the lawn to where her ball had come to rest, next to a small pond. Sitting on lily pads were three green frogs. 'Rivett!' they said, as though they were saying 'Hello!' to her.

Flora knelt and gazed at the frogs. The frogs gazed back. They looked as though they were smiling. The sight made Flora smile too. Then the frogs jumped, one after another. Up they went, with their long legs trailing and each frog spangled with silvery drops of water from the pond.

Flora thought of the little bag of spangles which lay in her mother's sewing box. 'I could have spangles on my frog costume,' she said to herself. 'How wonderful to be a spangled frog, jumping high in the air!'

'...but my frog's in the tree!' she said.

Flora ran back to her house. 'He's in the tree! I thought I could sew spangles on him, but he's in the tree… !'

Tears ran down her face and she hiccuped.

'Spangles?' said Flora's mother.

'In a tree?' said Flora's Aunt Jo.

'My frog,' said Flora. 'I threw him into a tree.'

She rubbed her wet cheeks and gazed at her mother and aunt.

'Everyone else was something nice, and I was just a frog,' she said. 'I didn't want to be one and then I saw some real ones with spangles…'

'Frogs?' asked Flora's mother. Flora nodded. Tears began to roll
down her cheeks once more.
'I know just how you feel,' said Aunt Jo. 'I didn't want to be an elf
until the bells were sewn on my shoes.'
'Blow!' said her mother, holding a tissue to Flora's nose.
'Come on,' she said, when Flora's face was dry. 'Let's go and get him.'

'I've come to take you home!' said
Flora, as she and her mother and
Aunt Jo ran into the school yard.
She jumped as high as she could,
grasped the frog's hand and gave it a
tug. Down he came, with his long
arms falling over her shoulders, as
though he were giving her a hug.
'Oh frog…' she said. 'I shall love
being a frog!'

Then all three hurried home, to sew on his spangles.

Acclaim for *Flora the Frog*

'A charming, expressively illustrated tale' *Book Fest, Ireland*

Enjoy more great picture books from Bloomsbury ...

   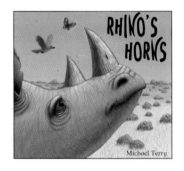

Grandma's Beach
Rosalind Beardshaw

Run, Rabbit, Run
Christine Morton & Eleanor Taylor

Whoever's Heard of
a Hibernating Pig
Shen Roddie & Eleanor Taylor

Rhino's Horns
Michael Terry